I Wish I Was an Alien

First published 2005
Evans Brothers Limited
2A Portman Mansions
Chiltern St
London W1U 6NR

British Library Cataloguing in Publication Data

 French, Vivian
        I wish I was an alien. - (Zig zags)
        1. Children's stories - Pictorial works
        I. Title
        823.9'14 [J]

ISBN 0 237 52851 7

Printed in China by WKT Company Limited

Series Editor: Nick Turpin
Design: Robert Walster
Production: Jenny Mulvanny
Series Consultant: Gill Matthews

ZIG ZAG

I Wish I Was an Alien

by Vivian French

illustrated by Lisa Williams

Evans

I wish I was an alien floating up in space.

I wouldn't wash my face.

7

...and I'd zoom around the stars.

I wish I was a boy on Earth
and didn't live in space.
I wouldn't have these
tentacles, instead I'd
have a face.

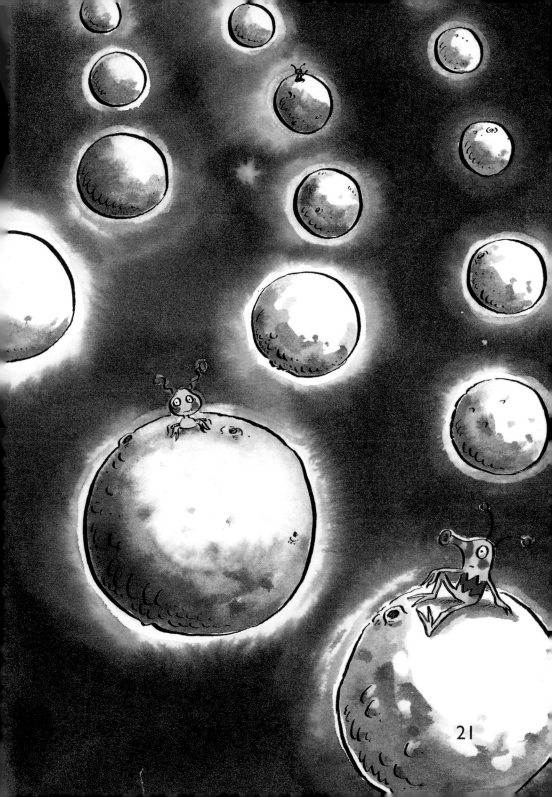

23

25

26

...and I want to go to school.

29

30

Why not try reading another ZigZag book?

Dinosaur Planet   ISBN 0 237 52793 6
by David Orme and Fabiano Fiorin

Tall Tilly   ISBN 0 237 52794 4
by Jillian Powell and Tim Archbold

Batty Betty's Spells   ISBN 0 237 52795 2
by Hilary Robinson and Belinda Worsley

The Thirsty Moose   ISBN 0 237 52792 8
by David Orme and Mike Gordon

The Clumsy Cow   ISBN 0 237 52790 1
by Julia Moffatt and Lisa Williams

Open Wide!   ISBN 0 237 52791 X
by Julia Moffatt and Anni Axworthy

Too Small   ISBN 0 237 52777 4
by Kay Woodward and Deborah van de Leijgraaf

I Wish I Was An Alien   ISBN 0 237 52776 6
by Vivian French and Lisa Williams

The Disappearing Cheese   ISBN 0 237 52775 8
by Paul Harrison and Ruth Rivers

Terry the Flying Turtle   ISBN 0 237 52774 X
by Anna Wilson and Mike Gordon

Pet To School Day   ISBN 0 237 52773 1
by Hilary Robinson and Tim Archbold

The Cat in the Coat   ISBN 0 237 52772 3
by Vivian French and Alison Bartlett